To: Raya
From: ShilohSanders

Tia'tynisha Adolphus

JULY 9, 1983-
JANUARY 10, 2012

For my mom,
Tia'tynisha M. Adolphus
July 1983-January 2012

Shiloh's very name bespeaks the gravitas and depth of her soul. Through a child's eyes she is able to see what many of us spend a lifetime blind to: The quiet strength of a broken heart. Not only should every child have a copy of *Shiloh's Prayer*, but so should every adult.

- Dr. Kenneth T. Whalum, Jr.,
and Sheila Whalum

www.mascotbooks.com

Shiloh's Prayer

For more information, please contact:
Mascot Books
560 Herndon Parkway #120
Herndon, VA 20170
info@mascotbooks.com

CPSIA Code: PRT0314A
ISBN-10: 1620865912
ISBN-13: 9781620865910

Printed in the United States

SHILOH'S PRAYER

Shiloh Sanders

illustrated by
Jamal Higgenbottom

LOOK UP AND SEE THE SKY SO BLUE.

GOD IS SMILING DOWN ON YOU.

THE STARS WILL SPARKLE O SO BRIGHT.

THIS IS THE TIME
TO SAY GOODNIGHT.

WORSHIP AND KNOW
THAT'S WHAT GOD CRAVES.

HE HONORS THOSE WHO WILL OBEY.

NOW, YOU MUST BE BRAVE AND CLOSE YOUR EYES.

THE ANGELS APPLAUD
YOU IN THE SKY.

WHEN YOU AWAKE
AND SEE THE LIGHT...

...ANOTHER DREAM WILL COME TO LIFE.

AMEN

Photo by Kenneth Cummings

About the Author

Shiloh Marie Sanders, a seven-year-old student at Southwind Elementary School in Memphis, Tennessee, wanted to express her own style at bedtime with a modern day prayer. Shiloh's mother passed away a year ago to Lymphoma cancer and she wanted to remember their favorite nighttime ritual of prayer. With that said, she combined her prayer ritual with her learning of True Worship by The New Olivet Baptist Church and created this prayer.